Usborne First Experiences

Going to
the doctor

Anne Civardi
Illustrated by Stephen Cartwright

Language Consultant: Betty Root

There is a little yellow duck hiding on every page. Can you find it?

The Jays

This is the Jay family. Jenny has a sore throat and Jack has hurt his arm. They must go and see the doctor.

Mum rings the doctor

Mum rings Doctor Woody while Dad helps Jack to get dressed. "Ow," shouts Jack, "mind my arm, Dad."

The receptionist

At 10 o'clock, Mum takes the children to the doctor.
"I've hurt my arm," Jack says to the receptionist.

Checking the records

The receptionist looks at the Jays' medical records.
"It's time for Joey's inoculation," she reminds Mum.

In the waiting room

In the waiting room, Mum reads a book to Jenny.
Other people are waiting to see the doctor too.

Doctor Woody

Now it is the Jays' turn to see Doctor Woody. "Who shall I see first?" she says to them. "Me," says Jack.

Doctor Woody examines Jack

Doctor Woody looks at Jack's sore arm. "It's not broken," she says, "but you have a nasty bruise, Jack."

Jack's sling

She puts Jack's arm in a sling. "Just wear that for a few days," she tells him. "It will get better soon."

Doctor Woody checks Jenny

Doctor Woody checks Jenny next. First she looks down her throat with a torch. "It's very red," she says.

Then she examines Jenny's ears with a special instrument. "Your ears are fine," she tells Jenny.

The doctor listens to Jenny's chest with a stethoscope.
"Breathe in and out deeply, Jenny," she says, gently.

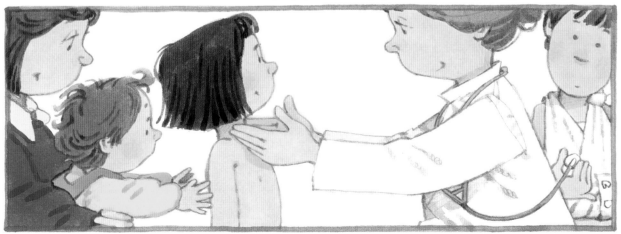

She feels Jenny's neck to see if her glands are swollen.
"You have a slight infection," she tells Jenny.

A prescription for Jenny

"Jenny needs some medicine," Doctor Woody tells Mum. Then she writes out a prescription.

Joey's inoculation

Now Joey has his inoculation. Doctor Woody gives him an injection in his arm. It hurts just a little.

To stop Joey getting polio, she gives him vaccine on a lump of sugar. Then she says goodbye to the Jays.

At the chemist

Mum stops at the chemist. She gives the pharmacist the prescription and he gives her some medicine.

Jenny goes to bed

At home, Mum puts Jenny to bed and gives her a
spoonful of medicine. "You'll be better soon," she says.

Dad comes home

Later, Dad comes home from work. "Look at my sling, Dad," says Jack. "We've all been to the doctor."

First published in 1988. This enlarged edition first published in 1992. Usborne Publishing Ltd, 83-85 Saffron Hill, London EC1N 8RT, England. © Usborne Publishing Ltd, 1992.